D0965630

A Note to Parents and Caregivers:

Read-it! Readers are for children who are just starting on the amazing road to reading. These beautiful books support both the acquisition of reading skills and the love of books.

The RED LEVEL presents familiar topics using common words and repeating sentence patterns.

The BLUE LEVEL presents new ideas using a larger vocabulary and varied sentence structure.

The YELLOW LEVEL presents more challenging ideas, a broad vocabulary, and wide variety in sentence structure.

The GREEN LEVEL presents more complex ideas, an extended vocabulary range, and expanded language structures.

When sharing a book with your child, read in short stretches, pausing often to talk about the pictures. Have your child turn the pages and point to the pictures and familiar words. Be sure to reread favorite stories or parts of stories.

There is no right or wrong way to share books with children. Find time to read with your child, and pass on the legacy of literacy.

Adria F. Klein, Ph.D.
Professor Emeritus
California State University
San Bernardino, California

Managing Editor: Bob Temple
Creative Director: Terri Foley
Editor: Peggy Henrikson
Editorial Adviser: Andrea Cascardi
Copy Editor: Laurie Kahn
Designer: Nathan Gassman
Page production: Picture Window Books
The illustrations in this book were rendered with watercolor.

Picture Window Books
5115 Excelsior Boulevard
Suite 232
Minneapolis, MN 55416
1-877-845-8392
www.picturewindowbooks.com

Printed in the United States of America.

Library of Congress Cataloging-in-Publication Data
Blackaby, Susan.
The emperor's new clothes / by Hans Christian Andersen ; adapted by
Susan Blackaby ; illustrated by Charlene DeLage.
p. cm. — (Read-it! readers fairy tales)
Summary: Two rascals sell a vain emperor an invisible suit of clothes.
ISBN 1-4048-0224-X
[1. Fairy tales.] I. DeLage, Charlene, 1944– ill. II. Andersen, H. C.
(Hans Christian), 1805–1875. Kejserens nye klþder. English. III. Title.
IV. Series.
PZ8.B5595 Em 2003
[E]—dc21
                                                        2003006111

The Emperor's New Clothes

by Hans Christian Andersen

Adapted by
Susan Blackaby

Illustrated by
Charlene DeLage

Special thanks to our advisers for their expertise:
Adria F. Klein, Ph.D.
Professor Emeritus, California State University
San Bernardino, California

Kathy Baxter, M.A.
Former Coordinator of Children's Services
Anoka County (Minnesota) Library

Susan Kesselring, M.A.
Literacy Educator
Rosemount-Apple Valley-Eagan (Minnesota) School District

PICTURE WINDOW BOOKS
Minneapolis, Minnesota

Long ago, there lived an emperor.
He loved clothes. He spent all of his
money on new outfits. He had a coat
for every hour of the day.

The emperor lived in a busy city.
One day, two men came to town.
One was a cheat. The other was
a fake. They were quite a pair!

The men said they made the finest cloth on earth. No other weavers made such flashy patterns in such bright colors.

"That's not all," said the fake. "Our cloth is special. Fools can't see it!"

"This cloth could come in handy," thought the emperor. He paid the weavers three big sacks of gold. "Make me an outfit," he said.

The weavers set up a workshop.
They ordered lots of fine silk thread—
but they hid it. From morning till
night, they pretended to weave
on empty looms!

The emperor was dying to look at the cloth, but what if he couldn't see it? If he was a fool, no one must know. "I'll send my adviser," he thought. "He's as clever as a cat."

11

The adviser visited the workshop.

He squinted hard at the looms.

He didn't see a snip or a scrap.

Of course the adviser couldn't see
the cloth. There *was* no cloth!
But he didn't dare admit he
couldn't see anything. "I must be
a blockhead!" he thought.

"What do you think of these rich shades of red?" asked the cheat. "Don't you love the diamond pattern?" asked the fake.

"Oh, yes!" said the adviser. "I've never seen anything quite like it. The emperor will get a full report."

The weavers were given more money
and supplies. The pretend weaving
went on night and day.

By and by, the emperor sent a duke to check on the weavers. The duke peered at the empty looms.

"I'm not a featherbrain," thought
the duke. "But I can't see the cloth,
so I must be a flop at my job!
No one must know." Out loud
he said, "What beautiful cloth!"

"How can I describe it?" asked the duke. The weavers told him all about the cloth. He passed the details on to the emperor.

Word of the fine cloth spread all through the city. The emperor had to see it for himself.

The emperor, his adviser, and
the duke went to the workshop.
Each thought the others could see
the cloth on the empty looms.

"Look at the bright shade of red,"
said the adviser.
"Look at the pattern of diamonds,"
said the duke.

"Uh-oh," thought the emperor.

"Am I a fool? I can't see the cloth!"

"Do you like it?" asked the cheat.

"It's fantastic!" said the emperor.
"You can wear it in the grand
parade," the adviser told him.
"Good plan," replied the duke.

"Perfect!" The emperor clapped
his hands. "You two are
the best weavers in the land.
Keep up the good work."

Snip! Stitch! Zip! The weavers
pretended to work like crazy.
At last they said the outfit was ready.
But the emperor couldn't see a thing!

The weavers pretended to dress
the emperor in his new outfit.
"It feels like a cloud! You won't even
know you have it on," said the fake.

The emperor looked in the mirror.
"A perfect fit!" said the cheat.
"The pattern and colors are so
exciting!" added the fake.

The emperor led the parade.
His adviser and the duke
pretended to carry the train
of his cape. People cheered
so they wouldn't look like fools.

Finally, a child spoke up. "Look!" he cried. "The emperor has nothing on!" Soon everyone was shouting. "The emperor has no clothes!"

"I've been tricked!" thought the emperor. "I *am* a fool!" But he held his head high and led the parade through the rest of the city.

Levels for *Read-it!* Readers

Blue Level

Little Red Riding Hood, by Maggie Moore 1-4048-0064-6
The Goose that Laid the Golden Egg, by Mark White 1-4048-0219-3
The Three Little Pigs, by Maggie Moore 1-4048-0071-9

Yellow Level

Cinderella, by Barrie Wade 1-4048-0052-2
Goldilocks and the Three Bears, by Barrie Wade 1-4048-0057-3
Jack and the Beanstalk, by Maggie Moore 1-4048-0059-X
The Ant and the Grasshopper, by Mark White 1-4048-0217-7
The Fox and the Grapes, by Mark White 1-4048-0218-5
The Three Billy Goats Gruff, by Barrie Wade 1-4048-0070-0
The Tortoise and the Hare, by Mark White 1-4048-0215-0
The Wolf in Sheep's Clothing, by Mark White 1-4048-0220-7

Green Level

The Emperor's New Clothes, adapted by Susan Blackaby 1-4048-0224- X
The Lion and the Mouse, by Mark White 1-4048-0216-9
The Little Mermaid, adapted by Susan Blackaby 1-4048-0221-5
The Princess and the Pea, adapted by Susan Blackaby 1-4048-0223-1
The Steadfast Tin Soldier, adapted by Susan Blackaby 1-4048-0226-6
The Ugly Duckling, adapted by Susan Blackaby 1-4048-0222-3
Thumbelina, adapted by Susan Blackaby 1-4048-0225-8